HOLT CLARKE

SANTA CLAUS

and the

KINGDOM of CHRISTMAS

Cover Art and Chapter Illustrations by APRILILY

Imagination 2 Creation Publishing

Charleston, SC USA

Books by Imagination 2 Creation Publishing may be ordered through booksellers or by contacting:

Imagination 2 Creation Publishing
www.HoltClarke.com

ISBN 978-0-9969791-6-0

To Alexis, Kiera, and Luke.

I love you!

"…for it is good to be children sometimes,

and never better than at Christmas,

when its mighty Founder was a child himself."

~ Charles Dickens, *A Chrismas Carol*

Also Available As An Audiobook

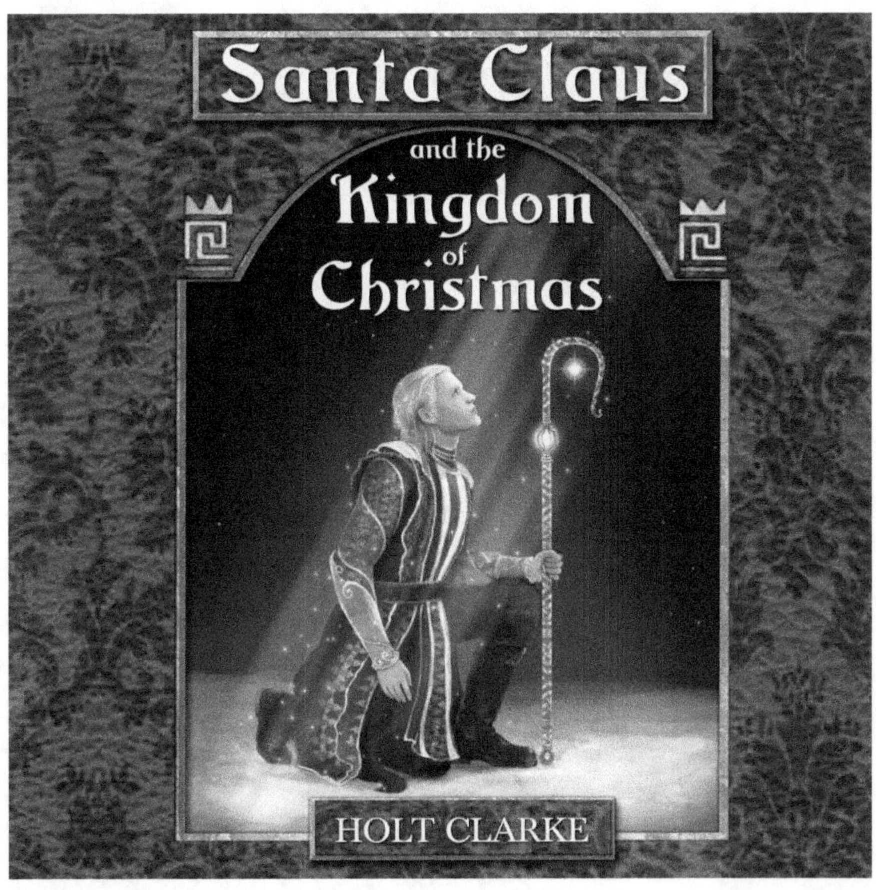

Chapter 1

SANTA'S DREAM

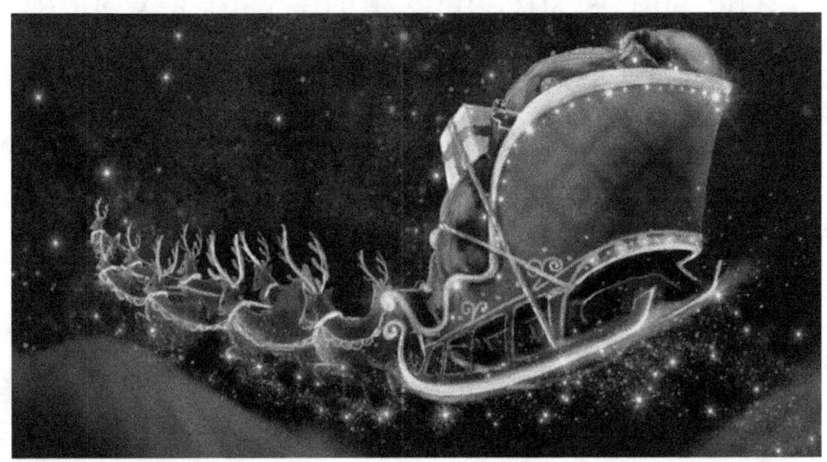

YOUNG SANTA CLAUS stood on Merry Hill, gripping tightly the Scepter of Christmas Magic. Gazing across the Great Sea, his silvery white hair blew behind him in the gusty winds. The distant caws of seagulls could be heard as Santa watched the sunrise casting its pearly light over the horizon.

Waves were rhythmically rolling up onto the shore below. Embers in the campfires interspersed along the hillside were still glowing hot. Santa gazed reflectively, recalling the vivid dream that had awakened him.

"The sun is stretching forth with a wondrous smile," Derya said, approaching from behind.

"Shifting snow drifts and darting reindeer – you startled me," Santa said with a flinch.

"Startled the winter dust off you did I?" Derya giggled.

"Oh, you most certainly did," Santa laughed. "But it's good that you did. I was thinking about a dream that woke me during the night. It was one of those dreams you wish you could remain forever."

"I love those kind of dreams," Derya replied. "What did you dream about?"

"We sailed far across the Great Sea aboard a ship with three large white sails. Arriving at a seaside port of ice, we continued our journey on foot to the North Lands. But much of the dream was fragmented," Santa said. "The images come and go."

"I hate when that happens," Derya said, twitching her pointed elf ears.

"But what I do remember, is the breath-taking beauty of the North Lands. And there were the most magical and delightful creatures you could ever imagine."

"Magical creatures you say," Rudimas said, strolling up. "More magical than our flight over Merry Mountain last night?"

"Good morning to you shining one," Santa said smiling. "These creatures looked just like the reindeer carving Derya gave me. And they could fly even though they didn't have wings."

"Maybe they are angelic reindeer belonging to Tinsel and the Christmas angels," Rudimas said, heartily clapping Santa on the back.

"Could be," Santa said reflectively.

"I was joking," Rudimas replied, noticing Santa was seriously considering the possibility.

"But your words may have merit," Santa said, before allowing a jolly smile to break across his face. "If we've learned anything this Christmas, it's that anything is possible where Christmas magic abounds."

"Look?!" Derya said excitedly. "There's the ship you described from your dream!"

The magnificent ship looked every bit a Christmas vessel. The keel was red with shimmering silver around the port holes, and black rails curving around the ship. The white sails billowed in the brisk wind as it sailed into Merry Harbor before dropping anchor.

Santa could hardly believe what he was seeing. "Well I'll be a reindeer's uncle," Santa said. "There she sails right out of my dreams and into the harbor. It's a sign."

"Well, look at that will you. The colors on that

ship are matching your suit ho, ho, Boy," Rudimas said with a chuckle.

"Whoever designed that ship certainly has a Christmas imagination," Derya said, twitching her ears.

"A Christmas vessel fitting for a Christmas journey," Santa replied, looking on with a mixture of fascination and excitement.

"So does this mean that we're going to jump on board and sail to the North Lands?" Rudimas said jokingly.

"That's exactly what we're going to do," Santa said with a glint of adventure in his eyes.

"Umm, seriously?" Rudimas replied with a raised eyebrow.

"By jolly Christmas, that ship is here for us and we are not going to keep her waiting," Santa gestured merrily toward the seafaring vessel.

"What about the others?" Derya asked. "Should I go get them?"

"Speaking of the sleepy heads, here they come now," Santa pointed as the rest of his merry band of Christmas companions strolled lazily down Merry Hill.

"Why is everyone up so early?" Praniel said yawning lazily.

"Because we are going on an adventure with Santa over the Great Sea," Derya said excitedly.

"You've got to be kidding!" Dansar said looking out over the vast expanse of the Great Sea that seemed to go on forever.

"That we are, my merry friends and we are setting sail with the outgoing tide," Santa grinned heartily.

"Where is Dunder?" Derya asked looking around.

"Good question?" Cubyt added.

"Knowing Dunder, he's probably already on the ship," Derya replied glancing over toward the harbor.

"Well then, let's not keep Dunder waiting. Let's get to the ship before he can say, jolly holly, my folly!" Santa exclaimed, as he darted off down toward the ship.

"Last one aboard cleans the deck," Rudimas hollered over his shoulder as he zipped off.

Before the words were barely out of his mouth, Derya took off in a sprint. "I love a race!" she hollered, hot on his heels.

"I'm definitely not cleaning the deck?" Dashire said as he flew with the speed of the wind down the hill toward the ship.

The rest of the merry band of Christmas companions wasted no time dashing down the hill.

Chapter 2

THE SEA SHEPHERD

S ANTA AND DUNDER were already aboard the ship as the rest ran up the ramp.

"What took you so long?" Santa said to Vixie-Rae with a guffaw.

"Very funny!" Vixie-Rae replied.

"Santa Claus," a pirate-like voice called from behind.

Turning toward the one calling his name, Santa gazed upon a grey bearded man who possessed the look of a sea Captain. Wearing navy velvet trousers, crimson socks and black leather boots, a white ruffled shirt beneath a silver vest, a green sash around his waist; the sea rover raised his black leather hat bound with silver lace trimmed with a green feather.

"I don't believe I've had the pleasure of making your acquaintance," Santa replied.

"Where are me manners? I be Captain Kringle. I've sailed to these here shores in search of one possessing ye heart of Christmas!"

"Oh?" Santa said curiously. "And how would you have come about such knowledge?"

"By shimmering angels and whispering wind," said the old sea-dog. "The most beautiful apparition I ever laid me seafaring eyes upon came skipping along ye waves. Pointed me to this here harbor, said I'd find a jolly soul dressed in a red suit who goes by the name of Santa Claus. And lo and behold, that I have. Right pleased I am to meet ye," Captain Kringle said, beaming smartly.

"Was this apparition dressed in blue with silver hair?" Santa asked.

"That she was, with hair shimmering brilliantly in moonlight," Captain Kringle replied. "A dazzling specter that stirred me imagination, that one did. Quite a time since I clapped me eyes on such a wonder. Charming and lovely she was. Yes siree, charming and lovely."

"That was no apparition. You were visited by the Christmas angel. Her name is Tinsel!" Santa exclaimed.

"Shiver me timbers, a Christmas angel, ye say. Then by living thunder we shall sail with the winds of heaven at our backs," Captain Kringle smiled. "Provisions are loaded; all is ready. Welcome aboard the Sea Shepherd!"

Santa looked around to make sure all were

accounted for: Rudimas, Derya, Dashire, Vixie-Rae, Blizha, Coamė, Praniel, Dansar, Cubyt, and Dunder. "All are aboard and awaiting your command Captain Kringle," Santa said.

"All hands look alive! Hoist ye sails! Shipmates and bold adventurers all! Set course for ye North Lands," Captain Kringle commanded ardently. "We're agoing adventuring!"

The sails caught wind as the keel sliced through the waves carrying Santa and his merry band of Christmas companions on a journey of discovery to the North Lands.

Chapter 3

SONG OF THE SEA

THE SEA SHEPHERD SAILED toward the golden sun peaking over the distant horizon of the Great Sea. The wind blew briskly making for a frigid dawn.

It wasn't long into the voyage before friends beneath the sea emerged. The first to appear was a pod of white dolphins at play near the bow of the ship. One white dolphin with emerald eyes, leapt out of the water while flipping in the air before darting back down beneath the surface.

"Did you see that?" Coamé yelled to the others excitedly.

Running across the deck of the Sea Shepherd, Dashire leaned over the bulwark trying to get a glimpse of the dolphins at play. Dunder reached over with his staff and pulled Dashire's feet out from beneath him, causing him to nearly fall overboard.

"Whoa!" Dashire called out, gripping the side of the ship steadying himself. Hitting the deck and whirling around with cat-like reflexes, Dashire locked eyes with Dunder who stood smiling.

"Be careful that you don't lean so far over that you find yourself swimming with the dolphin," Dunder said with a laugh.

"I'll keep that in mind," Dashire replied sarcastically. "You just keep that staff of yours away from my feet."

A day and a night passed before the first of several towering icebergs floated by the Sea Shepherd. Whistling away without a care in the world, Santa walked over with Captain Kringle joining the others who were warming themselves around an old iron barrel with a blazing fire licking up into the air.

"The temps are dropping quickly," Rudimas said.

"Aye, and they will drop even more as we draw closer to ye North Lands. We should be making landfall soon," Captain Kringle replied.

The most enchanting sound began coming from the sea, taking the chill out of the air. Everyone standing on the deck ceased their chatter as the sound inspired the most peaceful feeling. It was like listening to a chorus of angels humming a celestial melody.

Clapping his hands, a couple crew hands came

forward rolling a barrel with the sound of liquid swashing about inside. Turning the barrel right side up, the crew hand unplugged a cork as steamy, hot chocolate pour forth into oaken mugs.

"Drink up, me hearties! And warm ye bellies," Captain Kringle exhorted.

The hot liquid was a welcome delight as the wind became more gusty and brisk the closer to the North Lands they sailed. Standing around the blazing fire, chatter quickly gave way to listening wonder, as the the most enchanting sound arose from the fathoms, kindling its own symphony.

"It's the Song of the Sea," Dunder said breaking the silence. It is said that the Song of the Sea is sung by the most magnificent and magical creature of the sea known as the White Leviathan of the North. To hear its enchanting song is to be granted magical powers."

"We now sail in magical waters," Captain Kringle muttered, swaying ever so slightly to the hypnotic sea-song. The glassy clarity of the sea revealed darting wonders beneath the frigid waters.

"It is written in the sacred writings that 'in the beginning the Spirit of Father Christmas hovered over the waters.' And so even now, the Spirit of Christmas stirs in our midst," Dunder said sagely, eyeing Captain Kringle with newfound interest.

Derya's pointy elf ears twitched at the sound as she gazed out into the night, her imagination stirring to life. "We are blessed among mortals to hear such a wondrous melody."

"Blessed indeed," Santa remarked.

Chapter 4

WINTER DUST

A WHITE POWDERY substance began falling around the Sea Shepherd. Mountainous peaks towered in the distance.

"Land ahoy!" Captain Kringle cried out. "We are nearing ye North Lands."

Ascending from below deck, Rudimas shivered

in the cold air. The white powder fell upon his face, but didn't have the cold, wet feeling that comes from snow. "This is some strange snow that falls here in the North Lands," Rudimas said fingering the powdery substance.

"That's because it's not snow," Dunder uttered. "It's winter dust."

"Winter what?" Rudimas asked scrunching his nose.

"So, the stories are true," Santa said. "Winter dust abounds in the North Lands."

"Winter dust seems to be only falling around the ship," Derya said pointing to the land where no evidence of winter dust was falling.

Santa looked over the bulwark and noticed something white rising from the depths below. Breaching the surface and sending waves sprawling forth over the bow of the ship was the White Leviathan of the North, a giant white whale. Winter dust billowed forth from its blowhole cascading all around in the air.

Shimmering water creatures darted into the air before splashing back into the Great Sea. Another leapt high into the air where it hovered briefly, smiling at Santa before diving back into the sea.

"What was that?" Vixie-Rae asked.

"She is a Naiad, a water spirit," Dunder answered. "But it is extremely rare to see one wander so far away from fresh water settings. A kiss from a Naiad grants one immortality."

"Immortality?" Vixie-Rae asked with an inquisitive look.

"It means to live forever," Dunder replied.

"You mean being able to have a fun, jolly, time forever and ever?!" Vixie-Rae asked excitedly.

"Yes, that's right," Dunder laughed. "That would be one way to think about it."

"Hey! Check Derya out everyone!" Dashire hollered.

Rising in the air, Derya was magically floating up

toward the top of the Sea Shepherd's sails blowing in the wind.

"This is so cool," Derya shouted with glee, before rushing down toward the White Leviathan of the Sea and lightly touching down on its massive head. The great whale blew more winter dust into the air as Derya ran across the length of its body giggling as she did so. "Come on everyone! This is so much fun!"

"Now, that is what I'm talking about!" Vixie-Rae exclaimed.

"Ho! Ho! Ho!" Santa laughed as he began rising in the air. Everyone joined in the aerial fun trying twists, turns, and flips in the air as they ran, skipped, and walked along the back of the White Leviathan of the Sea. It was a magical time, as winter dust fell generously around.

"You are right Dunder! The magic is real and it's in the air everywhere!" Derya said, as she arched up in the air before soaring back down toward the deck of the Sea Shepherd.

Captain Kringle took great delight in the fun and excitement, laughing heartily as he looked on. And then appearing in the distance were the towering white peaks of the North Lands.

"Land ahoy! All hands on deck," Captain Kringle shouted. "Father Christmas has seen fit to deliver us safely to lands of snow, ice, and magical wonders!"

Chapter 5

THE NORTH LANDS

CAPTAIN KRINGLE'S SEAFARING crew secured the Sea Shepherd to an iceberg and heaved a wooden plank across for Santa and his merry band of Christmas companions to disembark.

"Yonder peaks is ye gateway to Christmas Mountain," Captain Kringle said, gesturing toward a towering mountain blanketed in snow.

"Thank you, Captain Kringle," Santa said gratefully. "You are always welcome at our hearth, where you will find warmth enough from kind, welcoming hearts."

"Father Christmas speed ye on yer journey and good fortune attend ye. May the fair winds keep ye always," Captain Kringle said heartily.

Santa and his adventurous companions stepped off the ship and stood on the compact snow, captivated by a vast, sprawling horizon of ice and snow as far as the eye could see.

The surface of the snow was like crystals refracting the dazzling light of the sun. In the distance, towering mountain peaks could be seen reaching high into the sky.

"So this is the North Lands," Derya said, breaking the lingering silence.

"We are going to need lots of winter dust if we are going to survive out here," Dansar said drearily.

"That's a lot of snow and a lot of cold," Rudimas said shivering, as he stared ahead at mounds of snow drifts beneath twirling and swirling white powder, dancing in harmony with the cold wind.

"I think I'll hang back with Captain Kringle on the warm ship," Praniel said as he turned to walk back to the ship before drawing up short, mystified by what his eyes saw or rather didn't see.

"Where did the Sea Shepherd go? Praniel said fretfully.

Santa along with the others strained their eyes in scanning the expansive horizon of the Great Sea. There was no sign of Captain Kringle or the Sea Shepherd anywhere.

"Truly Christmas magic surrounds us," Santa said, feeling the vibrant energy coursing through the scepter in his hand.

"I sense the spirit of Father Christmas stirring in this place," Dunder said, leaning on his rowan staff.

And then Santa saw the sign he was looking for as a light gleamed from within the entrance of mountain cavern; an illumination that triggered an energy surge in the scepter.

"There," Santa said, pointing toward the cavern. "Let us make haste to follow the beckoning light."

Santa hurriedly trudged onward through the snow following a hunch that warmed him inside out, the closer he drew to the distant light.

Dansar and Praniel just looked at each other with a "you got to be kidding me" expression on their faces.

"At least he's heading toward a cave that will get us out of the cold," Rudimas said, darting after Santa.

"Looks like a brilliant idea to me," Derya said, wasting no time sprinting off behind Rudimas.

"There is no fun, jolly time to be had standing here," Dunder said, lifting his rowan staff as the emerald stone gleamed to life. "Our destination lies ahead!" The others fell in step behind him, as their meandering thoughts turned to what further encounters awaited them along the frigid journey ahead

Chapter 6

FROSTGIFT

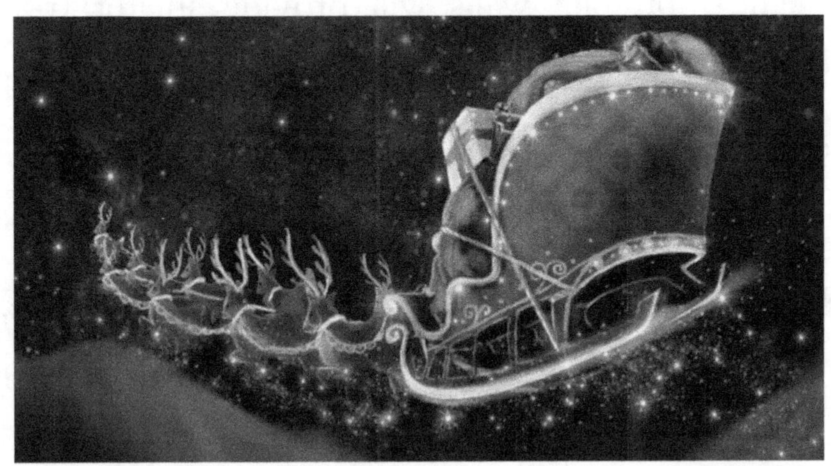

THE FAINT SOUND of a distant drum beat could be heard as the winds howled above the sprawling mountain range. Two snow peaks like sentinels, loomed overhead, with turrets of ice trailing along the icy ridge.

It wasn't long before Santa and his merry band of Christmas companions arrived at the mountain cavern that was shrouded in mystery. Santa approached a wall of darkness that marked the cavern's entrance. Peering into the void beyond, Santa shuddered as he gripped more tightly his scepter.

The mountain walls will provide shelter from the blustery winds," Dunder said, stepping up behind Santa, sensing his apprehension.

And then Dunder saw why Santa was not moving a muscle. Not more than a few feet away was a white snow beast appearing from the dark void.

"Is that what I think it is?" Dashire asked.

"Well, what do you think I am?" The white snow beast replied.

"It talks!" Derya belted in surprise, taking two steps back.

Santa raised his hand signaling for everyone to remain calm. He had a hunch about the white snow beast standing in front of them on its hind legs.

There was something friendly about its gaze.

"Of course I talk," the white snow beast remarked matter-of-factly.

Dashire looked to Dunder and then over at Santa for their reactions.

Leaning forward on his knotty rowan staff, Dunder said, "You must be the legendary Beast of the North."

"And right you are," the white snow beast answered. "But my friends call me, 'Frostgift'."

"You look like a polar bear," Dashire said.

"Well, maybe a polar bear looks like me," Frostgift replied raising his snowbrow.

"Merry Christmas Frostgift!" Santa said cheerfully. "We humbly seek your blessing, as we traverse the North Lands."

"The North Lands?" Frostgift replied. "We refer to it around here as the North Pole. It's as far north as one can get."

"What have you come seeking?" Frostgift asked.

"We are chasing a dream," Santa said.

"A dream you say?" Frostgift said, dropping down on all fours. "Dreams can be fast and elusive. Like trying to catch the wind, it is. Tell me? Are you determined to catch this dream you're chasing?"

"The dream we pursue is a dream awaiting the animating breath of Father Christmas, at which time it will welcome its first dawn," Santa said resolutely.

"Ah!" Frostgift intoned softly. "You pursue the dream whispered on the wind."

"Yes!" Santa exclaimed. "You know her voice?"

"Know her voice?!" Frostgift exclaimed. "Why of course I know her voice. It is the voice of Christmas angels borne upon the wings of the four winds."

"The dream we pursue holds at its heart the hope and promise of a kingdom of peace, hope, and joy, for all creatures great and small," Santa beamed.

"You're dream will surely inspire peace on earth and you shall bring good will to all people, shall you bring. Continue your journey by way of this cave, it will lead you to Christmas Mountain. May Father Christmas speed you on your way," Frostgift said.

And then inhaling deeply, Frostgift blew forth a mighty spirit wind. Santa and his merry band of Christmas companions fell backwards in the snow, blown over by the spirit breath.

Derya spun over several times before she was able to catch her balance and pop back upright. The others laid in the snow, dazed by the sheer force of the warm breath.

Dunder was the only one who remained standing able to maintain his balance by leaning into the spirit breath, absorbing the magical energy that flowed forth.

When Santa opened his eyes, Frostgift was nowhere to be seen.

Chapter 7

PASSAGE OF LIGHT

THE CAVERN WALLS dazzled the eye with iridescent light. Santa ran his hand over the icy wall encasing a variety of stones and gems glistening inside, creating a prism of Christmas colors.

The sound of ringing bells from down the cavern passage could be heard. Snowflakes began falling inside the cavern along with winter dust as bright white light from farther in the cavern illumined.

"I have never seen it snow inside a cavern before," Cubyt said while taking in the strange sight.

"Well, I've never been inside a cavern, so it's all the same to me," Praniel replied.

Two tall shadows danced ahead on the cavern wall growing taller by the moment. "What is that?!" Dashire asked apprehensively, drawing to an abrupt stop.

"Ring aling, bing bing," a squeaky voice said in the distance.

"I don't think he will like that song," another squeaky voice replied.

"Well, what jing aling thing do you think we should sing?" the first voice asked in exasperation.

Santa raised his hand signaling for silence as he slowly crept around the bend in the cavern. The others tip toed along in the crunchy, hard-packed snow before stopping to peep around the corner.

"Maybe something more like, bing aling, jing jing, jang," the second squeaky voice said.

"Don't like it! It's too…" the squeaky voice suddenly stopped as it eyes locked onto Santa's. "Jjjj," it said.

"Jjjj, what then?" the other squeaky voice said, before turning its large twitching ears toward what had captured his friends attention.

"Well, I'll be a jing aling," the squeaky voice said excitedly. "He's here!"

Everyone slowly stepped out from behind Santa, surprised to see that the tall shadows belonged to two white snow mice with squeaky voices.

"Look!" Derya said. "They're so cute."

"I am…" Santa started before the squeaky voice finished his sentence.

"Santa Claus! We all know who you are," the snow mouse said, leaping up onto an ice stump.

"Welcome to the Passage of Light. I am Ringle

and this is Tingle," the snow mouse said, twitching it's white whiskers while pointing to his snow white companion.

"I can introduce myself thank you," Tingle said, hopping up on the ice stump before giving Santa a curtsy. "I'm Tingle and I have a jangle for you."

"She calls a jingle a jangle," Ringle said rolling his eyes. "It's how she got the name 'Tingle' because she always likes to bring it."

"Bring what?" Santa asked curiously.

"Why a jangle of course!" Tingle said excitedly. "I love to bring a sing and watch believing hearts ring!"

"She believes her jangle of a jingle will make you feel a tingle," Ringle said.

"It will, I tell you. It will!" Tingle said enthusiastically.

"Oh?! Why, of course it will!" Santa said with a jolly smile. "By all means, let's hear your jingle…I mean jangle."

Clearing her voice, Tingle began squeaking very loudly, "Ring aling, bing bing, we jing and sing, so as to welcome you, oh Christmas king."

"Ho! Ho! Ho! My snowy friends." Santa cackled. "It is a Christmassy jangle of a jingle! And most delightful to the ear."

"I told you he would like it," Tingle said, rolling her little beady eyes at Ringle.

"We can certainly sing it again for you as a duet!" Ringle said scampering next to Tingle.

"We are most anxious to be on our way to Christmas Mountain," Santa replied with a jolly smile.

"To get to Christmas mountain, you will want to first meet Rolurth the Bright. Take you to him, we will!" Ringle said as he excitedly hopped down from the ice stump. Tingle scurried down after him as they both zipped on toward the bright white light ahead.

"Let's not keep our guides waiting," Santa

smiled to the others.

"Talking snow mice, a snow talking bear, a white whale blowing winter dust, and a vanishing ship along with its sea captain. This journey is getting stranger by the minute," Dashire said.

"Strange can be good, especially when Christmas magic lingers in the air," Dunder said, lifting his rowan staff and walking ahead.

Stepping into the Passage of Light, everyone followed closely behind Santa. But there was no sign of Ringle and Tingle anywhere. It was as if they had vanished into thin air.

Chapter 8

ROLURTH THE BRIGHT

REACHING THE END of the Passage of Light, Santa was about to step forward when he felt a hand grab his shoulder. "You might want to rethink your next step," Dunder cautioned. Santa held his foot in the air, face turning ashen white as he peered over a cliff ledge; a white chute of snow dropped off into a never-ending chasm below.

A sky-piercing sound gave everyone a start, as a shadow careened by, air whooshing past, flinging loose snow up in its wake.

"What in the jolly holly was that?" Rudimas cried out.

"All I saw was a white shadowy figure," Dashire said.

"It's a flying reindeer!" Derya marveled, pointing to the magical creature circling back in the sky toward them. "Just like the one in my dream."

"Ho! Ho! Ho!" Santa belted merrily. "Well, I'll be a jolly holly."

The magnificent reindeer soared through a drifting cloud bank, gracefully galloping in the air. The resplendent creature was white as snow with eyes as blue as the midwinter sky. It dashed forth as if running on the snowy earth.

Dipping down toward the mountain ledge, the reindeer lifted its head back as it came in for a landing not far from where Santa was standing. Sounds of clicking and clopping on the snow echoed around the mountain.

"Welcome to Christmas Ridge," the majestic reindeer said, bowing its head low before Santa. "I am Rolurth the Bright."

"I am…" Santa started to say, before Rolurth the Bright finished his introduction.

"Santa Claus. I am honored to be at your service," Rolurth the Bright said, lifting his head adorned with a grand rack of antlers.

"We are here to take you and your companions safely across to Christmas Mountain," Rolurth the Bright said.

"We?" Santa asked looking around.

Rolurth the Bright belted forth a thunderous call. It wasn't the typical oinking pig sound that reindeer usually make. No sooner had the sound escaped Rolurth the Bright's mouth, several reindeer soared down to land.

A reindeer for each adventurer clicked and clopped through the crunchy snow along the snowy ledge. Derya was overcome with excitement as she immediately jumped up onto the back of a reindeer.

"Nice to meet you as well, young one," the reindeer said to Derya. "I am Lumya."

"And I am Derya. Our names sound alike!"

"That makes us special friends," Lumya said with an endearing smile.

"Well then," Rolurth the Bright began. "Let us be on our way to Christmas Mountain." Following his lead, all the reindeer knelt down so a rider could climb up and straddle their back.

"Now let us soar upon the Christmas winds!" Rolurth the Bright proclaimed. And as one, all the reindeer took to the clouds, soaring over to Christmas Mountain.

Santa clung tightly to the reigns around Rolurth the Bright's neck. For as far as the eye could see, Santa was amazed at all he saw. More magical creatures appeared on the ground and in the air.

A white dragon with the most radiant green eyes soared up from the misty void below and rolled past Santa with a wave. "Merry Christmas Santa," the white dragon said.

"Merry Christmas!" Santa replied. "I'm really starting to dig this place," Santa said amusingly to Rolurth the Bright.

Glancing off to his right, Santa saw a polar bear running along an approaching mountain peak as it leaped into the air heading straight for him.

"Merry Christmas Santa!" The polar bear said, saluting as she floated past lazily in the air.

Chapter 9

FATHER CHRISTMAS

SOARING OVER THE first peak of Christmas Mountain, the most spectacular view greeted Santa's eyes. A breath-taking vista held the rapt attention of everyone. Mountain peaks in the distance jutted up toward the heavens with majestic grace. An expansive valley spawled forth, covered in sparkling snow that razzled and dazzled in the pristine light of the sun.

The winter wonderland was teeming with animals frolicking and playing. Reindeer dashed and jumped about in a field of white fluff, playing reindeer games.

Penguins were waddling around while several sea lions scooted along hurriedly. Santa heard one sea lion say to a penguin, "Tag! You're it!" while lurching forward to slide down an icy slope.

"This place is incredible!" Rudimas yelled.

"Oh, you think?!" Coamé replied playfully.

"Hey Rudimas, check out the reindeer down yonder with the glowing red nose!" Vixie-Rae hollered excitedly.

"A reindeer after my own heart," Rudimas chuckled merrily.

Rolurth the Bright touched down first as the other flying reindeer landed behind flanking his left and right in a v-formation. The assembled formation was not lost on the others. It was a call to gather.

Captivated by the sight of Santa Claus, all ceased their play and eagerly approached. Festive song and much gaiety could be heard from the distant heights. Santa turned toward the cheerful sounds and noticed two columns of what appeared to be small children streaming down the snowy slopes.

The first to approach was one who looked to be the leader of the most interesting band of little people. With sea-grey eyes, he looked Santa up and down before casting a quick glance at the others.

As if giving his approval he said, "Welcome to Christmas Mountain most honored among us. I am Dimly the Dreamer." And gesturing to the others gathered behind him, "We are the Elves of Christmas, charged with nurturing dreams from imagination to creation."

"Thank you most kind Drimly. Dreams are a most powerful form of Christmas magic. I stand inspired!" Santa said, bowing his head in kind respect and affirmation.

Stepping before Derya, the elf approached to examine her more closely. "You are the face in my dream, most imaginative one. We are at your service," Drimly said, with a slight bow of his head.

Derya suddenly felt self-conscious in being addressed in such a way. She respectfully nodded her head with a smile, "It is I who stand ready to serve."

"Then we shall serve together," Drimly said with much spirit. "May the jolly smile of Father Christmas be with us, each and every one!"

Santa felt a stirring inside as he saw in Drimly's gaze, an ancient mystique that led him to believe that the Elves of Christmas were much older than they appeared.

"We come to you from afar, guided by the Spirit of Father Christmas. And that makes us kindred spirits," Santa said. Looking to the others he added, "We are all one in purpose, brought together by the

Spirit of Christmas."

A Christmas cheer went up by all. Rolurth the Bright snorted in excitement blowing forth winter dust in the air.

Santa saw before him the fulfillment of his dream on Christmas Mountain. The glint of the sun above refracted off his brilliant blue eyes

"This is a place where dreams can take root and grow," Derya said.

"Yes, indeed." Santa said, sensing a potent Christmas magic, stirring in a powerful way among the land, the animals, and the people. And then the most brilliant light appeared within swirling winter dust before slowly forming the appearance of a man.

The mysterious figure arrayed in garments of pristine white with silver accents gazed at Santa with penetrating eyes as brilliant as the stars. Winter-white haired draped his shoulders matching his flowing beard, giving him the look of an ancient prophet. A north wind ruffled the white flowing cloak draped behind him.

The ancient one possessed a happy, light, and cheerful demeanor. To look into the ancient one's galaxy-blue eyes was like gazing into the eternal heavens.

"Do not be alarmed my friends," the ancient one said. "Each of you have been summoned to this place, endowed with gifts. In time, you will hone these gifts and spread them around the world." Hearts were uplifted and comforted at the sound of his voice.

"And it will spring forth from here," he said, sweeping his arms around the entire lay of the land. "Behold the Kingdom of Christmas!"

Christmas mountain clapped in reverberating applause, echoing the thunderous voice of the ancient one. The pristine snow upon the stone-cold earth, sparkled like a thousand diamonds blessed with an inner fire. Nature bowed in radiant wonder.

Chapter 10

KINGDOM OF CHRISTMAS

THE SCEPTER OF Christmas Magic shimmered in Santa's hand. The stone near the crook began to glow in a bright, incandescent white light. An energy coursed through Santa's body.

The world itself went silent as Santa felt himself drift into a dream-like state. The scepter glowed even brighter, vibrating in his hand, as if beckoning to him. "What do you see?" the scepter spoke in Santa's mind.

Gazing around at all that his eyes beheld, Santa replied, "Beautiful mountains and a snow covered valley."

"No, what do you see?" the voice probed, sounding like that of the ancient one in Santa's mind. Looking over to the ancient one standing by his side Santa, his galaxy blue eyes teeming with winter dust. The others gathered around were all staring at the valley ahead as if transfixed by a mysterious wonder.

Santa closed his eyes and tried to recall the dream that had awakened him prior to the journey. And then it all came back to him.

"Now take the Scepter of Christmas Magic and throw it with all your might to the valley below," the voice within instructed.

Santa opened his eyes and lifted high the scepter

as it glistened with magical power. Drawing back, he summoned all the strength he could muster and threw the scepter. It soared through the air like a javelin carried by the wind much further than Santa thought possible before it struck the cold earth with a surge of energy.

The valley floor shook like a volcano about to erupt. And then the ground splintered as earth, snow, trees, and fire merged in a magical dance teeming with winter dust.

"Now call forth your dream and unleash your imagination," a voice commanded.

No sooner had Santa called forth his dream with vivid clarity, a sprawling Christmas palace with towers clawed forth out of the snowy tundra and ascended in majestic grandeur toward the heights.

Village shops and several toy factories appeared, lining streets made of rock crystal. A crystal-blue river twisted along through the enchanted village, burbling and bouncing along with a watery grace beneath several quaint bridges.

Appearing along the ridge of Christmas Mountain were Christmas angels with majestic wings of energy spreading forth in glorious light. Several among them began to play instruments of flute, lyre, and harp; creating intoxicating sounds that reverberated among the valley. The melodious sound enchanted the imagination as Father Christmas swayed in delight.

Santa and his merry band of Christmas companions felt transported by the melodious sounds. Dancing along the ridge line were Ringle and Tingle, Frostgift, Rolurth the Bright, and Captain Kringle. Gusting winds swooshed down the mountain ridge scattering winter dust all around.

And then a castle of ice and snow began to assume form as the wind churned and spun with such force before revealing three spiraling towers and a silver dome that glistened in the sunlight. A glittering silver bridge hung over a babbling and burbling river that swept around the castle.

"A castle that never melts and yet ever warms both heart and hearth," Santa said, gazing in awe at what his imagination had brought into existence. "Only in dreams did I ever believe such a kingdom could exist."

"It's so beautiful!" Derya said, stepping up next to Santa. "A place where imagination has no limits and creativity can inspire a joyful world."

"And a magic that moves mountains and creates wonders to behold," Santa muttered, gazing incredulously upon a transformed valley that only moments before was a frozen tundra of snow drifts and iced over river beds."

"It's all teeming with winter dust," Dunder observed.

"What is winter dust?" Rudimas asked curiously.

"It is the breath of Father Christmas, the essence of the magic that fashions and sustains all that your eyes behold," Dunder sagely answered.

"Who are you?" Santa asked to the ancient one, with a strong suspicion of the answer.

"Many names am I called. Here at the North Pole, I'm known as Captain Kringle, White Leviathan of the North, Frostgift, Ringle and Tingle, and Rolurth the Bright. I am known among the angelic host as Father Christmas!" The ancient one boomed merrily, his voice echoing around Christmas Mountain.

"The North Pole," Santa repeated, recalling the words of Frostgift, as the dawn of realization swept over Santa. He knelt down on bended knee, bowing his head as the others did the same.

"We are humbled to be in your presence," Santa said, head still bowed before Father Christmas.

"Please rise," Father Christmas said, wearing a megawatt smile.

Santa stood to his feet noticing the stars above sparkling like angel fire. Gazing into the eyes of Father Christmas, Santa felt a stirring within, as if drawing from the energy of eternity itself. The spirit of Christmas kindled within him, burning as bright as star flame.

"Welcome to your new home," Father Christmas gestured, waving his hand around the expansive valley below. "The Kingdom of Christmas welcomes its king. Serve her well for in so doing, her magic will spread to all."

Scampering over to stand next to Father Christmas, were the Elves of Christmas. "And these are helpers of Derya's ilk," Father Christmas said winking at Derya. "They have a special ability to harness the power of dreams and bring them to life. They will serve you well."

Father Christmas closed his eyes once again while swaying in the stirring wind that began whirling around them, teeming with Winter Dust. Like the evanescent beauty of a sunset, Father Christmas shimmered in crystalline light before vanishing into the whistling wind. Winter Dust swirled where he once stood before swooshing off toward the snowy mountain peaks above.

Magically materializing before Santa, was a magnificent sleigh arrayed in colors of red, silver, and gold. Piled on the back were sacks filled with toys and gifts ready to be delivered.

Enchanted by its stunning appeal, Santa looked upon the gleaming sleigh like a child taking that first peak under the Christmas tree on Christmas morning.

"Well, go ahead," Drimly said tugging at Santa's suit. "Climb on board and watch what happens!"

"You heard him," Santa said looking at the others. "Let's climb on board."

Santa and his merry band of Christmas companions all clambered on the sleigh leaving no room to spare. Drimly whistled as nine reindeer quickly assumed positions out in front of the sleigh.

Drimly gazed at Santa and said, "Now all you have to say is the magic word."

Rearing back with the most jolly smile, Santa began quaking with laughter as the spirit of Christmas washed over him. "Ho! Ho! Ho!" he proclaimed. "Merry Christmas!"

Barely had the words escaped his lips when the reindeer in perfect unison, lurched effortlessly forward, climbing up and away, toward the flashing and flickering stars above.

Santa Claus gazed at the brilliant stars, glittering like sparks of angel fire; beacons of hope for the poor, destitute, and abandoned. For soaring with him, was the hope and promise of the Kingdom of Christmas.

THE END

Visit HoltClarke.com

Visit HoltClarke.com

Visit Holtclarke.com

Visit KieraClarke.com

Visit KieraClarke.com

ABOUT THE AUTHOR

Holt Clarke is the father of the coolest kids on earth, on Santa's Nice List, and keep'n the magic real with his family in Charleston, South Carolina.

Holt earned the Doctor of Ministry degree from Drew University, Master of Divinity degree from Duke University, and Bachelor of Arts degree from North Carolina Wesleyan College.

Visit HoltClarke.com for news and updates.

SPONSORED BY

SUPPORTING THE LITERARY ARTS

CharlestonianProperties.com

www.ingramcontent.com/pod-product-compliance
Lightning Source LLC
Chambersburg PA
CBHW071013120726
47910CB00004B/1498